RAILROAD!

A Story of the Transcontinental Railroad

by Darice Bailer

Illustrated by Bill Farnsworth

Little®
Soundprints

Published by Soundprints Division of Trudy Corporation, Norwalk, Connecticut.

Book design: Marcin D. Pilchowski
Editor: Laura Gates Galvin
Editorial assistance: Chelsea Shriver

First Edition 2003
10 9 8 7 6 5 4 3 2 1
Printed in China

Acknowledgments:
        Soundprints would like to thank Ellen Nanney and Robyn Bissette at the Smithsonian Institution's Office of Product Development and Licensing for their help in the creation of this book.

Library of Congress Cataloging-in-Publication Data is on file with the publisher and the Library of Congress.

Table of Contents

A note to the reader:

Throughout this story you will see words in **bold letters**. There is more information about these words in the glossary. The glossary is in the back of the book.

Chapter 1
Say Cheese!

"Stop fooling around!" Lucy cries. She's trying to take a picture of her best friends, Tomas, Emma and Kevin. They are standing in front of a long, green steam locomotive in the Transportation Hall at the Smithsonian Institution's National Museum of American History. Instead of smiling, Lucy's friends are acting crazy. Just as Lucy is about to snap a picture, Kevin holds up two fingers behind Emma's head. He is trying to give her rabbit ears.

"Cut it out, Kevin! These pictures are for the school paper!" Lucy pleads.

Suddenly, the sound of a steam locomotive screeching to a halt fills the room. Lucy jumps at the sound. She drops her camera and it crashes to the floor. Lucy looks around to see what made the noise. It was only a recording from a nearby exhibit. Lucy's friends run off for a better look.

"Now I'll never get a picture," sighs Lucy.

As she picks up the camera, a large drawing inside a glass case catches her eye.

Lucy studies the drawing of men crowded around two old locomotives. The sketch looks very familiar. The information on the display case says the men are celebrating the completion of the First Transcontinental Railroad in 1869. Lucy reads about how the Central Pacific Railroad crews building east from California, met with the Union Pacific crews coming west from Nebraska to meet at Promontory Summit, Utah.

Suddenly, Lucy knows why the drawing looks so familiar. It's a sketch of a famous photograph taken by Andrew J. Russell. She's seen it in her history books at school!

"Well, if I can't get a picture of my friends for the school paper, I'll get a picture of this," Lucy says to herself. She puts her camera to her eye, but suddenly there is a cloth over her head! Lucy pulls the cloth off and looks around. There, standing in front of her are all the men from the sketch.

"What is going on?" gasps Lucy.

Chapter 2
History in the Making

"Mr. Russell, are you ready to make the photograph?" someone in the crowd asks Lucy.

"Mr. Russell? I'm not Mr. Russell! I'm Lucy!" she cries. But it's no use. The crowd is loud and nobody hears her.

Lucy wonders why they think she's Mr. Russell. She looks down and realizes she is not wearing her regular clothes. She is now wearing baggy pants and stiff boots—she is dressed like a man!

"They really think I am the photographer," Lucy whispers to herself. "Hey, this could be fun."

Just then, a man tips his hat to Lucy. "Good day, Mr. Russell. I'm so glad you'll be photographing this event. It's hard to believe the last **spike** of the railroad will be laid today!"

Lucy smiles. She lowers her voice to sound like a man. "I am honored to be here. The photograph I am about to make will be published in history books for years to come." Lucy giggles to herself. She is quite sure of that!

Lucy looks at the strange camera in front of her. Luckily, she knows a lot about photography. She's read that old cameras didn't use film. The photographers had to mix chemicals and pour them over a glass plate. The glass plate then turned into a negative that could be used to print a picture on paper.

Lucy looks over at a wagon that is near her. It must be Mr. Russell's! She climbs up to look inside. As Lucy looks around, she realizes this must be A.J. Russell's traveling **darkroom**. She looks for the things she'll need for the photograph.

Outside the wagon, Lucy hears two men talking.

"Poor Theodore Judah," one man says. "It was his dream to build a railroad across the continent! He wanted to make travel easier through the West. It's sad that he died so young."

"Yes, the poor man died in 1863, the very same year this railroad was started."

Lucy agrees that it's very sad that Theodore Judah never lived to see his dream come true.

Chapter 3

Hard Labor

Lucy jumps down from the wagon. She is curious about the men who worked on the railroad. She sees two Chinese men with long braids. She walks up to them and introduces herself.

"Hello, gentlemen. My name is Andrew Russell."

"How do you do, Mr. Russell? My name is Yang Li and this is Long Ho. We work for the Central Pacific Railroad."

"How did you ever build the railroad through these mountains?" Lucy asks the men.

"Oh, it was very hard!" replies Mr. Li. "Sometimes it took all day to chip away a few inches with our picks and shovels. It took us three years to lay 100 miles of track through the **Sierras**!"

Lucy is amazed! She is about to ask why they didn't use a bulldozer or a digger, but she catches herself. There were no gasoline-powered machines back then. No wonder it took the workers so long to build the railroad!

Suddenly, Lucy notices Yang Li's right hand. He is missing his fingers!

Yang Li notices Lucy looking at his hand. "The **black powder** got them," he quietly tells her. "We were building the railroad along the cliffs above the American River Canyon. I drilled small holes in the rock and set blasting powder inside. Then, I would light the powder on fire and run to get away from the blast. Sometimes the powder exploded out of the hole like a cannon."

Lucy listens carefully to Yang Li's story. "Then what?" she asks.

Yang Li sighs. "One time the blast caught my hand before I could run away."

"I'm so sorry," Lucy tells Yang Li.

"There were many hard times," Long Ho says. "The winters nearly killed us!" he exclaims. "I remember one winter at Donner's Pass. You have never seen so much snow. It was piled forty feet high!"

Forty feet is taller than Lucy's house! School would be closed for weeks!

"It was very dangerous working in the snow. It was so soft that we would sink to our shoulders," Long Ho says. "And, there were many snowslides that buried people alive. We had to dig them out."

A group of workers from the Union Pacific gathers around Lucy, Yang Li and Long Ho.

One of the men says, "You think the snow was bad? You have no idea what we went through!"

Chapter 4

The Final Days

Yang Li holds up his hand and argues, "We had the Sierra Mountains to blast through! What could be worse than that?"

The man from the Union Pacific named Patrick replies, "Well, we had the Lakota-Sioux and Cheyenne Indians on the Great Plains of Nebraska."

Lucy remembers reading about the Indian raid at Plum Creek after the railroad pushed the Lakota-Sioux and Cheyenne Indians off their homeland.

Lucy realizes it must be very sad for the Indians to watch the railroad celebration. She knows it can't be much of a celebration for them.

Lucy wants to hear more stories, but she has to get to work. After all, what would happen if she didn't take the photograph?

Lucy dips the glass plate in a flat metal pan filled with chemicals. She overhears Patrick and another group of workers talking to a reporter.

"In the end, the Central Pacific and the Union Pacific were twenty-five miles apart and racing to the finish. Whichever railroad laid the most track would earn the most money," says a Central Pacific Railroad worker.

Everyone begins to gather for the driving of the last railroad spike. Lucy finishes preparing for the photograph just in time.

She looks out at the large group of workers. They all played such an important part in building this amazing railroad!

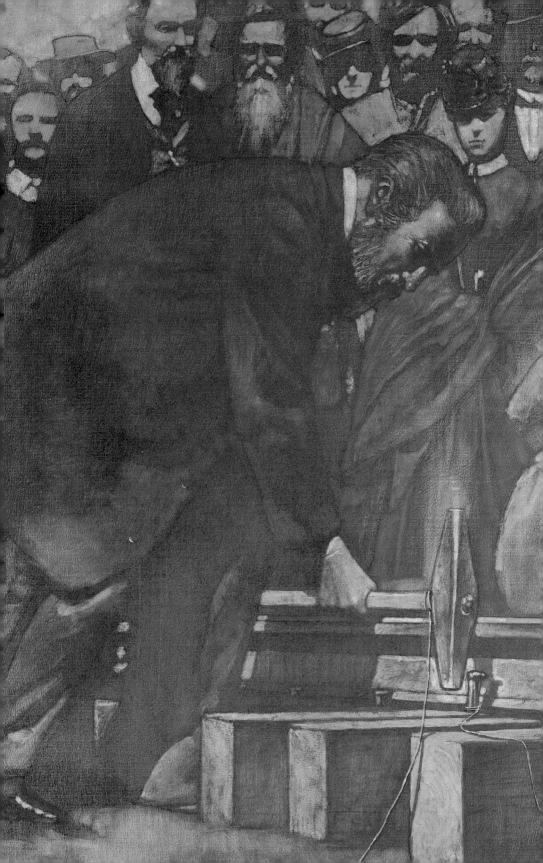

Chapter 5

Done!

Lucy lifts up her glass plate and the ceremony begins.

Mr. Leland Stanford, one of the owners of the Central Pacific Railroad, holds up a shiny golden spike. It is engraved with a message. Mr. Stanford reads it to the crowd: "May God continue the unity of our country as this railroad unites the two great oceans of the world."

The golden spike and another are gently tapped into a railroad **tie**. Then Mr. Stanford removes them for safekeeping.

Attached to Mr. Stanford's silver hammer is a wire leading to a **telegraph** on a nearby table. A telegraph operator sends a message to the rest of the country. "DONE," types the operator. The news flashes across the country.

The two locomotives move forward and touch.

Lucy's glass plate is set and she inserts it into the camera. "Get ready, everybody," she yells. "It took all of you almost six and a half years to build the railroad, but I just need thirty seconds to take the picture!"

She sticks her head under the dark cloth and opens the shutter to expose the negative. The picture has been taken!

Chapter 6

An Incredible Feat

Lucy pops out from behind the cloth. She is still in awe of the railroad. These workers left their families to go out and work in the wilderness. That wilderness is now open to people everywhere. The pioneers who travel west will be just like astronauts exploring outer space. People can now travel from coast to coast in just two weeks. New towns will be built and trade will move more freely, in this country and abroad.

Lucy closes her eyes. "What an incredible feat!" she says to herself.

Locomotive bells and whistles ring in the distance. Lucy opens her eyes.

"Where am I now?" she asks herself. She looks around. She is back in the museum staring at the sketch in the glass case.

Tomas stands beside Lucy. "This photo was taken by a guy named Andrew J. Russell," he tells the group.

He looks at Lucy. "It's a nice photo. I bet you could never take one like this!"

Lucy smiles to herself. If only Tomas knew!

Glossary

Black powder: explosive powder used for blasting.

Darkroom: a room without light that is used by photographers to develop and print photographs.

Sierras: the Sierra Nevada Mountains in California and Nevada.

Spike: a very large, specially shaped nail used to fasten the iron rails to the wooden railroad ties.

Telegraph: a device for sending messages by code and transmitting them electronically by wire.

Tie: a heavy timber of wood, laid on the ground, to which rails are fastened by spikes.

About the Transcontinental Railroad

Before 1869, there was no safe or easy way to travel across the United States. The chief engineer of the Sacramento Valley Railroad, Theodore Dehone Judah, planned to join the East and the West by building a Transcontinental Railroad.

Congress passed the Pacific Railroad Act of 1862, authorizing the Union Pacific Railroad to build a railroad westward from Omaha, Nebraska, and the Central Pacific Railroad Company to build a railroad eastward from Sacramento, California. The two companies were to meet somewhere in the middle.

Both railroads broke ground in 1863. On May 10, 1869, the two construction crews met at Promontory Summit in Utah. There they celebrated the joining of the nations first Transcontinental Railroad.

One day after the Golden Spike Ceremony, the first train traveled west. Soon, passengers and freight crossed the continent in less than two weeks. Eastern companies shipped tools and machinery out west, and western farmers shipped grain and cattle back east.

Travel from east to west was far easier, quicker and more comfortable than it had ever been. The nation was unified at last!